To family
pets
who have
gone.

Frank king of the dogs

Charlie dog, diagnosed as being allergic to himself

Tiger cat, mother of Max and Little Wet Wonder

Max disappeared

Little Wet Wonder went blind and walked off the deck

Banana duck, hit by a falling tree

Cheeky budgie

Tweety the budgie who fell off the perch

Mopsy goat

Mickey mouse, accidentally strangled

Harry dog, walked out the front door

Holly dog

Sparky dog, also known as Wiggins

Sylvester cat

Audrey cat

Yuki cat

Red the orange cat

Tom lizard

Leader chook

and chooks 1 and 2

Princess Ariel the fish that ate itself

Chris fish

The snails

Robot Chicken

SCARLETT and the Scratchy MOON

Dog

Chris McKimmie

Allen & Unwin

I CAN'T SLEEP. THE MOON IS MOVING AGAIN.

SCRI

IT'S SCRITCH SCRATCHING THE SKY.

SCR

SCRITCH SCRITCH

It's
Scratching
the SKY.

I'M BUSY COUNTING SHEEP.

one   two

DADDY NEEMA

MUMMY NEEMA

123

three

Baby
NEEMA

What's that?

ONE-TWO-cha-ch

the outside night?

-cha, ONE-TWO-CHA-CHA-CHA,
ONE-TWO-cha-cha-ch

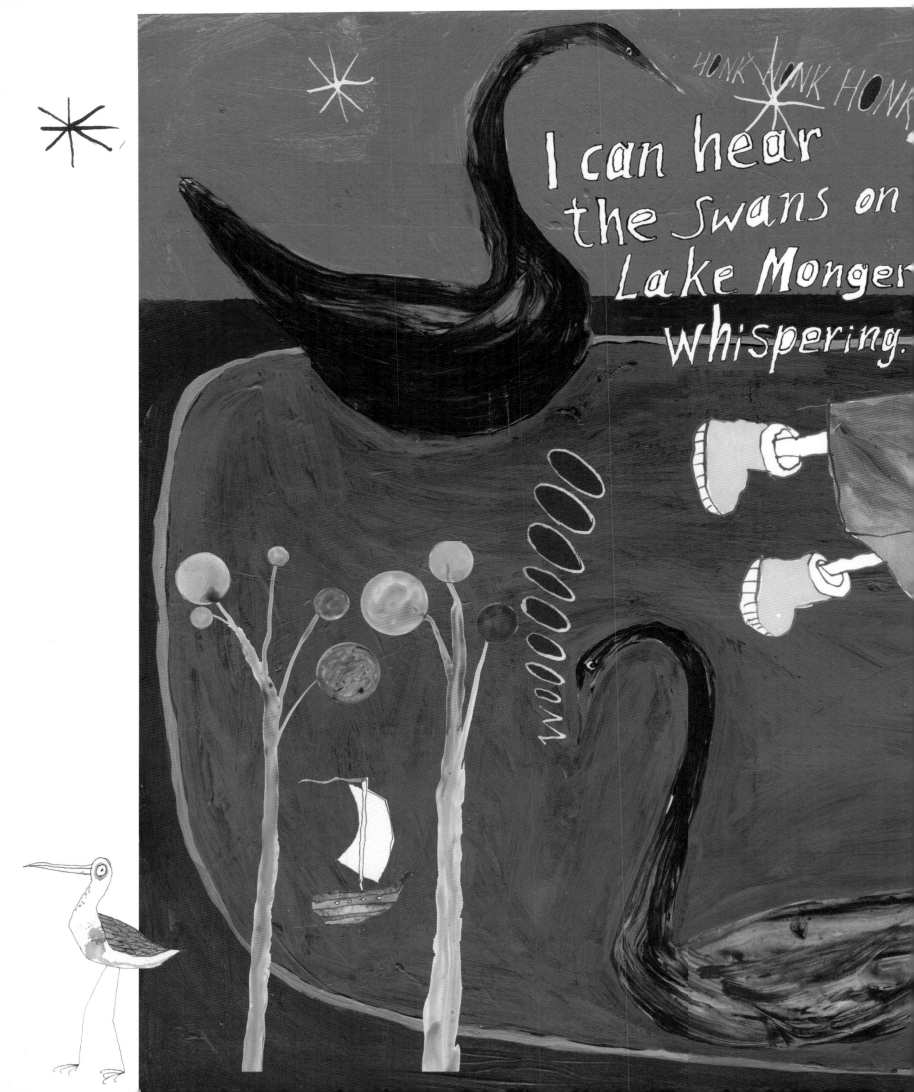

I can hear
the swans on
Lake Monger
whispering.

Ever
since
Holly
and
Sparky
died.

I had clouds in my eyes.

THE SUN COMES UP.

Wake Up! Get out of Bed!

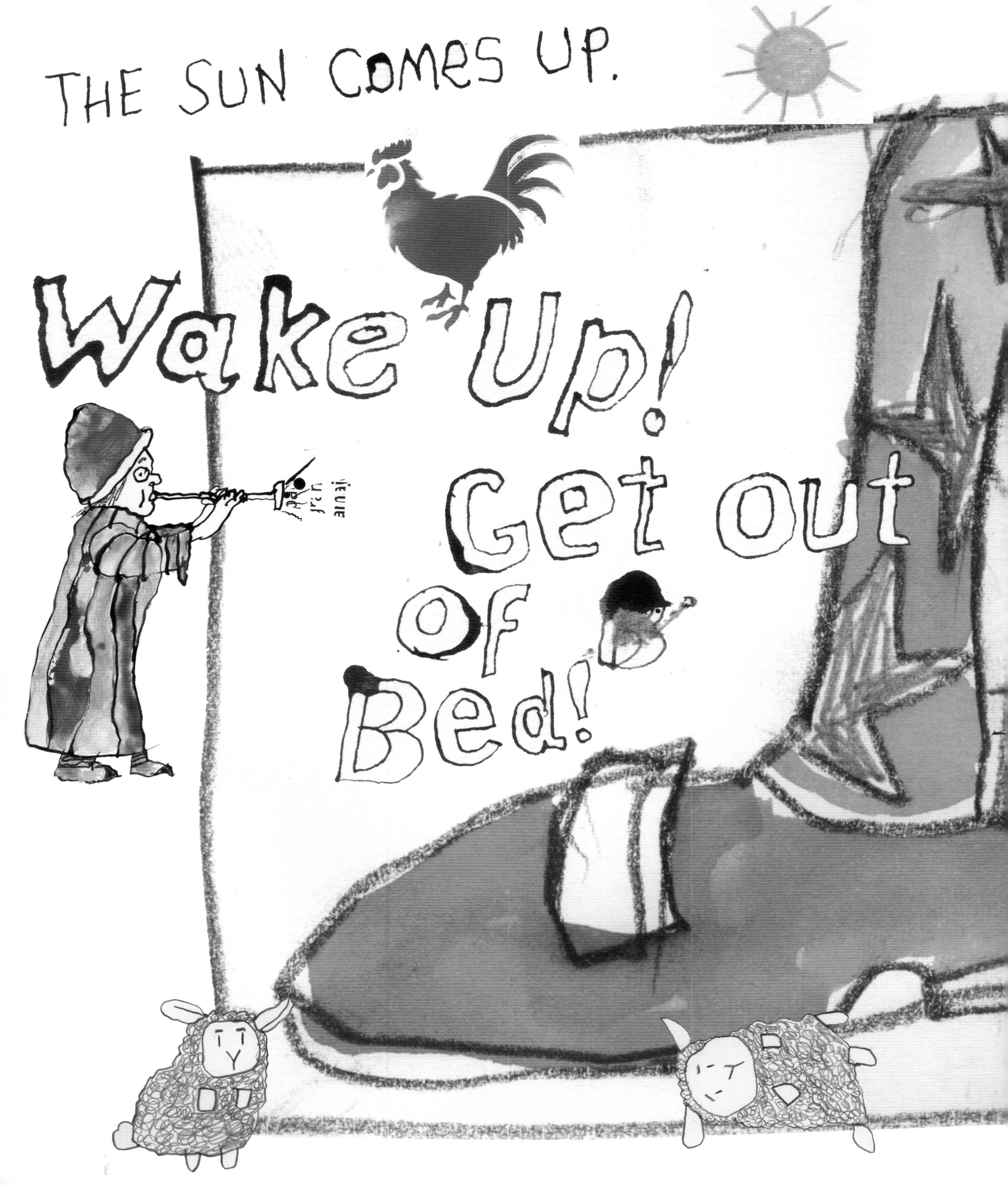

THE BIRDS START TALKING.

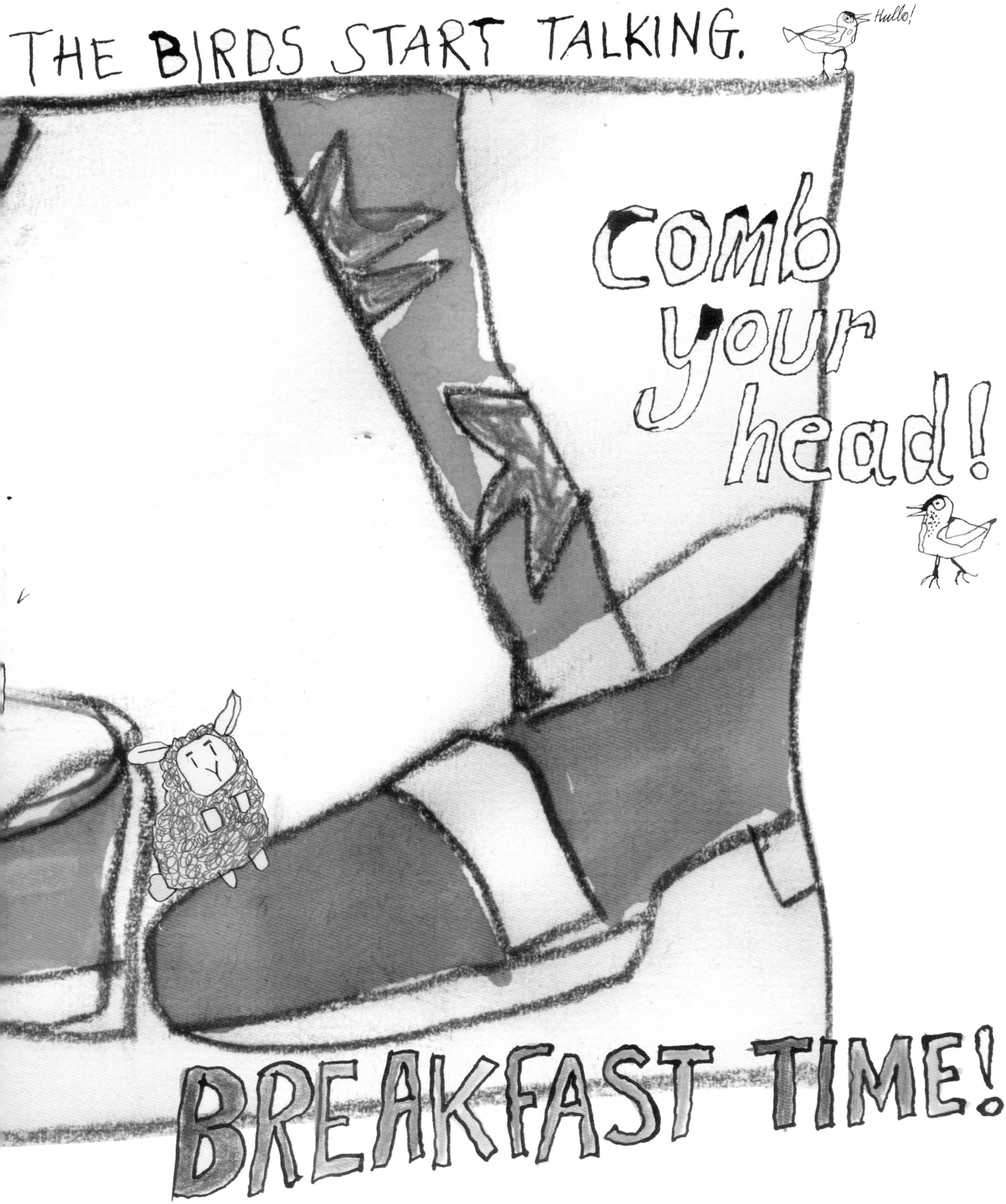

BREAKFAST TIME!

It must be something for me.

toot
toot
toot
toot

toot

MARCUS

tweet tweet tweet

WOO

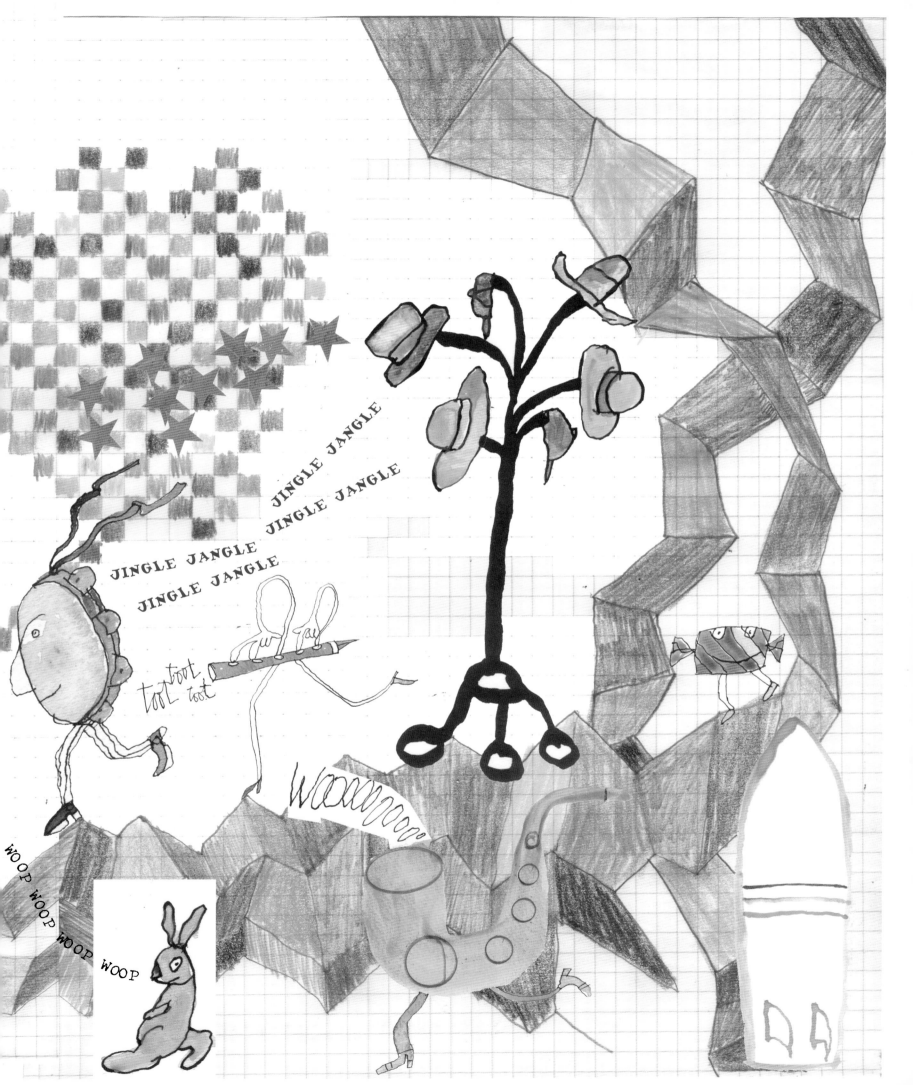

It is!

a Tiny Rex

WOOF!

A Harriett

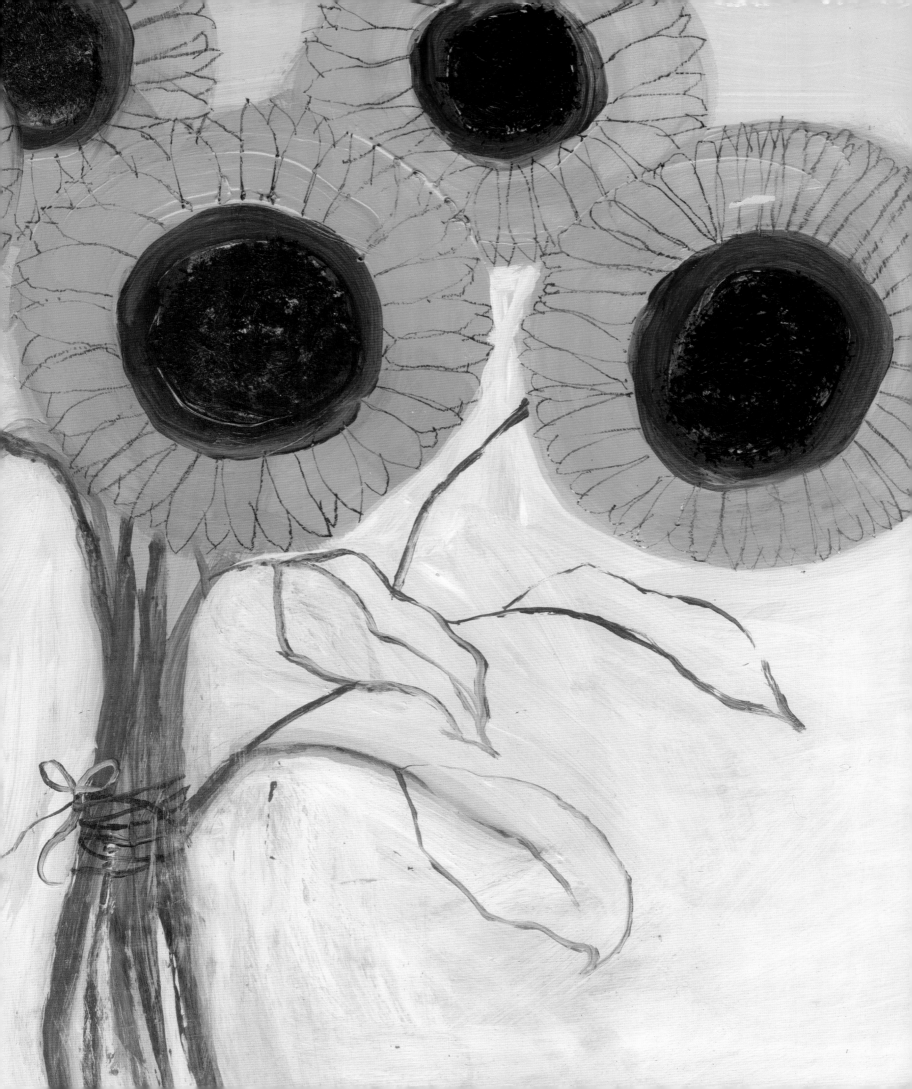

WARM AS TOASTY TIME.

Mummy Neema and Daddy Neema are fast asleep.

Someone is not in bed. Baby Neema!

Yo! WHO'S BEEN SLEEPING IN MY BED, BRO'?

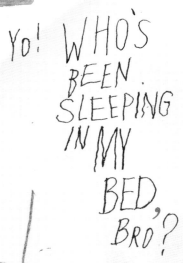

Goodnight.

First published in 2013   ISBN 9 781 74331 515 6

© Chris McKimmie

Copyright words and images 2013

Book design, cover design, lettering by Chris McKimmie

Dylan McKimmie,
Scarlett's father,
was an invaluable source of
anecdotes, information and
photographs for this book.

Thanks to
Jackie McKimmie for the
idea for the dedication page and
for everything else and
thanks, once again,
to
Erica and Susannah.

Lucy McKimmie (6)
did the drawing of
Sparky on the
title page.

Tiny Rex is also
known as Emmy.

Drawings on the second endpaper
were done by
Alex, Maisie, Lucy,
Dylan, Blake and Chris McKimmie.
The age they were
when they did
the drawing is
in brackets.
Audrey by Lucy (6)
Red by Maisie (6)
Heart by Alex (8)
Mopsy by Dylan (5)
Max by Dylan (5)
Tweety by Dylan (4)
Frank by Blake (15)
Cheeky by Blake (8)
Charlie by Blake (4)
The rest by Chris (66)

A Cataloguing-in- Publication entry is available from the
National Library of Australia www.trove.nla.gov.au

This book
was printed in
January 2013 at
TWP SDN BHD, TAMPOI
No.89 Jalan Tampoi
80350 Johor Bahru

10 9 8 7 6 5 4 3 2 1

allen & unwin

83 Alexander Street Crows Nest NSW
2065 Australia
phone: (61 2) 8425 0100
fax: (61 2) 9906 2218
e mail: info@allenandunwin.com
web: www.allenandunwin.com

TRACING PAPER
CHARCOAL
WATER COLOURS
ACRYLIC PAINT
PENCILS
LEAD CARBON
COLOURED
BUTTONS
PASTELS
PEN AND INK
GOUACHE
ACRYLIC INK
CARDBOARD
STENCILS
GAFFER TAPE
CONTE CRAYONS
MASKING TAPE
BAND AID

m.d.f board
canvas
board
felt pen
Gestetner
stencil.

Frank

Charlie

Red

water food

Princess Ariel

Sparky and Holly

Leader and chooks 1 and 2

Robot chicken